Dorm Game

a Brazen Boys story

by Daryl Banner

Books By Daryl Banner

Dorm Game: a Brazen Boys story

Copyright © 2015 by Daryl Banner

All rights reserved.

This book is a work of fiction.
Names, characters, groups, businesses, and incidents
either are the product of the author's imagination or are
used fictitiously. Any resemblance to actual places or
persons, living or dead, is entirely coincidental.

Cover & Interior Design : Daryl Banner

Cover Model : Nick Duffy
www.instagram.com/nickduffyfitness

Photo of Nick Duffy by Simon Barnes

Dorm Game

a Brazen Boys story

by Daryl Banner

[1]

I've found the world's greatest source of renewable energy, and it is horniness.

He waits for my answer. His eyes are dangerous and bright, two chips of ice in a hard, perfect as porcelain face. The devil plays on his lips and the belt hangs heavily from his right hand like a tail, a devil's tail. It's *his* belt. Somehow that makes this whole thing all the hotter. The sweat on his skin and the dim light shining from the lamp on his desk make his powerful pecs glow, smooth and shining, as he stands over my body tied down to the skinny dorm bed.

"What's your answer, boy?"

Andrew and I are both twenty and he calls me "boy". I told him not to do the "boy" thing when he first moved into my dorm, but Andrew isn't the type to follow orders. He made it clear from the start: *he's* in charge when we play the dorm game.

"Tell me your answer, unless you're *wanting* the punishment."

If I had known studying for tests would be this fun, I'd have had him move in the second we met.

"A," he asks, licking his lips, "or B?"

The right answer will earn my throbbing cock a few teasing, pleasurable strokes from his strong and all-too-clever fingers. The wrong answer ...

"R-Read the question again?" I beg.

His eyes narrow. Andrew looks so sexy when his eyes narrow. Especially wearing nothing but those loose, acid-washed jeans sagged just enough to show the black waistband of his boxers, the brand printed in giant green block letters across it. With a voice as hard and unforgiving as iron, he repeats the question patiently to me. He knows how deeply I'm breathing without even listening. I'd swear he even knows my heart rate, my thoughts. He knows the answer in my jagged sighs and can tell whether it's reward or punishment I crave. His strong jaw working to produce the words of the question, I'm distracted by the beauty of this boy I've let into my life, this boy who *drips* sexuality. He sweats and I'm horny. He rubs a spot on his shoulder and I'm hard in an instant. I've wanted Andrew for so long and now I have him.

Or perhaps it's more accurate to say, *he* has *me*. Fastened to a bed, at his total mercy, it's pretty fucking clear I'm not going anywhere.

The question is about the names of bones in the hand. It makes me wonder about the bones in *my* hand; the knee-length soccer socks he uses to tie me up constrict my wrists, cramping them in a strangely pleasurable way. I wonder, for as many times as we've done this, why the bones in my hand haven't broken from my pulling on them to escape his playful fingers and less playful lashes.

"A," I choose when he's finished.

He smiles coolly, then flips the flashcard. I see the answer circled. "Correct," he announces, then tosses the flashcard aside like nothing. The belt hanging from one hand, he lazily reaches the other toward my cock, and when the fingers squeeze to claim it, I suck in air. He strokes it once. He strokes it twice, then lets go.

"Don't stop," I beg, but I know better than to beg. My every ounce of pleasure is allowed or denied by his frisky hands. Literally. I'm starving to death and my cruel friend offers me crumbs. *Why do the appetizers make me so much hornier than the actual meal?* But this is who Andrew is and who I've become, and we are both expert players of the dorm game.

Casually, he brings the next card to his

face. "Ah," he mumbles. "A question about ... arms."

"I like arms," I say, wriggling against the binds.

"Oh?" He presses his lips together, clenching, then bends his arms into a perfect double-bicep pose. His veins pop. He grunts. "Like these ones?"

He does this on purpose. Knowing I can't reach my cock, that I can't jerk myself off while looking at his perfect baseballs-for-biceps ... It's agonizing.

"I want to cum so bad," I breathe.

He drops his arms and laughs at me. "Fourteen more to go," he says, "and then we'll consider it."

[2]

Andrew's always enjoyed being in control.
I met him in an Intro to Psychology class last
year when we were sophomores. The prof was
a total pushover and half the students slept,
even in the front row, but the sight of Andrew
kept me awake every day. He'd always sit near
the side, elbows propped on the desk so I'd get
this delicious view of his flexed triceps and
back muscles most of the hour. The way his
shirts fit tightly against his back, sucking on
his arms, painting his traps and bulged
shoulders, I'd find myself nursing a secret

hard-on so often that I can count on my hand the amount of classes I *wasn't* hard.

It became an obsession pretty quick. I would make sure to get to class super early just so I could excitedly anticipate him arriving. I'd sit in my desk and watch the door like a dog. The rustling of clothes and side conversations happening all around me were bothersome because it all tried to distract me from the sight of Andrew walking into class. When at last he arrived, I'd clench the edge of my desk—my hands already plenty sweaty—and study what he was wearing. Another tight shirt of some color or another. Tight jeans he squeezed his powerful thighs and thick jock butt into. I wondered what he did in high school. Was he a walking football quarterback wet dream? Cocky captain of the wrestling team? Bored too-much-time-on-his-hands weightlifter? Bully with four older brothers he had to grow stronger than?

Too soon, the class always ended, and all my classmates scattered like my memory of half the lesson I was supposed to be paying attention to. One of these countless days, I found a speck of courage and did what any normal person would do when consumed by a classroom crush.

I stalked him. As I didn't have another class for three hours, and I was miserably obsessed with Andrew, I went in the same direction he did, which was basically opposite of my dorm where I would otherwise be headed. Seemed his next destination was the math building, not far from the psych hall. I kept my distance and, moments after he went in, I then followed. I was certain he didn't know I was on his sexy tail.

Once in the building, I saw him disappear into the first auditorium, then realized that, in fact, I did *not* want to sit through an hour-long algebra class. Also, I was sorta creeping myself out with all this stalking. Feeling a stroke of panic lance down my arms, I gripped my backpack and turned on my heel, vacating the math building for good.

I shouldn't make a habit of this, I realized. *People do not like to be followed.* But for the next hour, I found myself helplessly glued to a bench near the exit of the math building. I was pretending to enjoy the sunshine, pretending to catch up on the last psych chapter, but every five seconds I'd glance up at the doors, wondering if I might catch Andrew leaving them. Every person that pushed through the door sent a jolt of excitement through me, even when it turned out not to be him.

Then suddenly, it was him.

I casually gathered my things and began to follow. Again. *What the actual* fuck *am I doing?* I continued down the path many, many, many paces behind him, and discovered with relief that he seemed to be headed to the food court. Just so happened, I was hungry as a motherfuck.

Of course, half an hour later found me seated on the opposite side of the commons, watching as he pushed a fat burger into his big, sexy lips. He was all by himself. No one sat with him. No one approached him. No one walked past to say hi. For some reason, the seeming lonesomeness of his character drew me in. I felt like I related to him, just in that solidarity factor, that ... *aloneness.* I wanted him to be just like me, somehow. I wanted all the obvious differences in our appearances to be nothing compared to some deep inner sameness about the two of us. *That isn't so improbable,* I reasoned, desperately hopeful.

Desperately horny.

Chewing on my lame, tasteless sandwich, I knew how stupid I sounded. *We're nothing alike,* I told myself, bitter, *nor will we ever be. You should go back to your dorm and your boring roommate and give up this creepy obsession of yours.* Still, I stayed there to watch him until the bitter, delicious end.

My roommate was going to move out the following year. That meant some random cat they pulled from the sophomore or junior bowl was going to be shoved into the vacancy in my room. Staring hungrily at Andrew across the food court, I wondered what it'd be like to be *his* roommate. Would we work out together? Would he be embarrassed of me? Maybe we could help each other study. Yes, I really, truly thought that, even then, sitting there with my sad sandwich and the dream boy within my view, not knowing a thing that my future would hold, I sat there and pondered a life with Andrew for a roommate.

He got up unceremoniously and moved to the trashcan with his empty bag of chips and a crumpled up napkin. I flinched, daring myself to follow, but half of my sandwich remained, and suddenly I lost the nerve to keep up with him. *Doesn't matter,* I thought, trying to comfort myself. *I'll see him Friday.* He walked toward the exit of the food court, shoved his way out of it, and the muscular walking orgasm was gone.

That night, as I rested in bed with my eyes to the ceiling and a textbook opened at my side that I'd given up on an hour ago, I listened to the gentle hum of my roommate talking to his girlfriend on a cellphone in the bathroom. For a moment it sounded like arguing, then it became pleading, and finally I heard the echoing ring of laughter.

Really, relationships are so strange to me. The only guy I'd ever been sexual with was some fruit ball my junior year of high school whose voice was two octaves higher than mine, but his hair was always done up really fucking amazingly. One day afterschool he'd insisted on coming over to "give me a makeover" or something, and I agreed even though I and the whole school knew he was gay. In the bathroom, he turned my hair into something half-amazing and half-scary, then grabbed my face with two oily palms and cried, "You're hot shit!" When I tried to thank him, he planted his lips on my face, and somewhere between the hairspray and two a.m., half a handjob and some clumsy kissing happened. The next day he told his two best girlfriends that we were boyfriends, and I denied it, and then there was an argument and a lot of ugly words were thrown around, and suddenly I had nothing to do anymore with him or anyone he knew. It was a very confusing and painful week.

I just never grasped the concept of boyfriends or lovers or whatever. My right hand sufficed.

And when my roommate finally got off the phone and mumbled something at me about staying at his girlfriend's that night, he threw a bag over his shoulder and took off. The room all to myself, I spent exactly twenty minutes reading the same sentence over and over again in the psych book before giving up, pulling up a porn site on my laptop, and feverishly searching for something that reminded me the most of Andrew. I settled on some puffy muscled guy flexing, then unzipped my pants. His face was all wrong and his shirt didn't fit him as tight as I wanted it to, but he pulled the thing off too soon anyway, and I jerked until the stars were traded for a wash of morning sunlight.

I was officially, irrevocably crushing hard on the muscle god from Psych. So, naturally, that Friday when the prof announced that we would be partnering up for a joint research paper and project, my stomach fell through the floor.

[3]

Excitement thundered into me like a horrid sickness and my legs turned to overcooked fettuccini. To my left, I saw boys partnering up. To my right, boys and girls and everyone partnering up. Straight ahead, Andrew sat there, bored, tight-shirted and muscular and ... *waiting*.

I couldn't believe it. No one was going for him and no one was approaching me. Maybe it's a fluke. Maybe I should wait. Maybe someone was headed for my desk right now and as soon as they'd ask, I'd weakly agree to be their partner while longingly staring at Andrew from across the classroom and swallowing all my what-ifs. What is it about a sick concoction of courage and horniness that drives us to do stupid things? Was I about to do the stupidest thing of all?

I was up from my seat and began to move. The world was falling to my left, falling to my right, and the classroom was a blur of noise and voice and colors. As I approached his desk, I felt myself getting sicker and sicker, shaking all over. *I've never been this nervous before,* I remember thinking. Still no one approached him. Why? Didn't anyone else see this beautiful hunk of beefsteak just waiting to be claimed?

Halfway to his desk, he turned. That's when our eyes connected for the first time in my life, and I stopped. He just sat there, fierce and beastly, his blue-steel eyes pinning me in place. He made no effort to move or get up, even while we stared at each other, both of us waiting—waiting for what?

He wanted me to finish my walk toward him. He wanted me to humiliate myself. Even this early on, teaching me that he always gets what he wants.

I started moving again. The rest of the walk to his desk took seven forevers. Walking toward him, he neither spoke nor smiled; he just sat there, his bright eyes locked on me, waiting, almost bored.

And then I was in front of his desk. He hardly made the effort to lift his chin. I felt the throbbing of my nervous system in my *fingertips* and if I didn't get the words out soon, I was going to faint.

"Do you ..." Already ran out of breath. I braced myself, noticed I had put a hand on his desk—perhaps to ensure that I wouldn't fall over—then finished: "Do you want to b-b-be partners?"

He regarded me lazily. The muscles in his shoulders flinched. His arms twitched deliciously as he shifted his body around to have a better look. I was breathing funny and my palms were so sweaty I thought they'd fall off.

After what might have been the length of a sentence to hell, he finally said, "Alright."

Oh fuck, his voice. Deep, smooth, strong. Involuntarily, I lowered into a seat next to him. I didn't even check to see if anyone was sitting in it and I'm super glad no one was because I'd be in their lap now. "Cool," I finally allowed myself to say, grabbing my fingers, unsure what to do with them, resting them on my thighs. "I'm Michael."

"Andrew," he said back, but of course I already knew that. Every day's roll call told me so, again and again: *Andrew Knudson*.

I took a second to peer across the rest of the class, surveying all the other partnerships that had been formed. I still couldn't believe no one else thought to approach Andrew. He had no friends in the class, I figured. Maybe he intimidated everyone else just as much. Maybe he was put in this class just for me.

I was self-centered and horny, I don't care.

"So?"

I returned my attention to him, realizing I was losing myself in my own head. "Yeah, okay," I said, bringing myself into focus. "So, uh … next we need to, uh … we need to figure out a subject for our paper."

"Yeah," he grunted, playing with a pencil in his hand. The way his fingers moved, making the pencil dance between them, among them, under and over them, I should've known right there how expert he could be with his fingers. *He has clever fingers. Wicked fingers. Playful fingers …*

"So … do *you* have any ideas for … um …?"

He shrugged his big muscular shoulders and focused his bright, cold eyes at the ceiling. I couldn't tell if he was in thought, or just so horribly uninterested that he was counting the minutes until class was over. *Was this a mistake?* I wondered. *Did I steal him away from someone else? Was he hoping some hot chick would've asked to pair with him?* I felt guilty instantly.

But despite my guilt, I also felt lucky as fuck. I felt special. I felt like I'd *won* something. Yeah, he's probably straight, and I had half a mind to sneer at all the girls that could've partnered with him, even the other dudes in class, anyone that could've come between me and the object of my desires. I had a sudden and hungry possessiveness take hold of me.

It was a game of partners and I'd won.

Noting his clear lack of enthusiasm for the tedium of work, I began to suggest ideas for our psychology project. Andrew was very, very little help. *He wants me to do all the work,* I realized, but somehow I wasn't annoyed by it. If the price of being within his proximity was doing the work, I'd pay it happily. I'd pay it all year long, just to make sure we're partners every time.

Of course, every idea I had Andrew shot down. "Dumb," he said to one. "Lame," he said to another. Then finally he cuts me off and says, "Games."

"Games?"

"The psych behind them," he said, a tinge of annoyance in his voice, as if I ought to have followed his train of thought perfectly with just the few unhelpful words. "Games we play."

"I don't get it. Video games?"

"You think I'm hot?"

My mouth was opened with my next words on my tongue, but his question froze me in place. A hundred thoughts raced through me and my heart was in my throat. Was he onto me? Did he, all this time, know that I was some horny, lonely, drooling guy in the back of the classroom waiting for this one sad moment to throw myself at him? Did he *know* I was stalking him that whole time, following him to math and then to the food court?

I realized even now, he could still decide not to be my partner and go find someone else. I could lose him.

"What—What—What do you mean?"

"You hoping this project's gonna get us close or something?" he asked, his voice so low I could swear his words were being submitted to me by telepathy. *He's inside my head,* I told myself. I was shaking so bad, I could feel my pulse in my fucking eyeballs. Still, he went on, almost gently: "Wanna touch me, Michael?"

"I don't—I don't know what you—why you—"

"I'm playing with you, get it?" His eyes burned with their furious hot-blue irises. "The games we play with each other. Teasing. Button-pushing."

"Oh. The ... the psychology of games," I said back, studying him uncertainly. Question was, was he *still* fucking with me, or was he serious? My pulse blinded me, making my eyesight unclear. I wondered if my vision was the only thing all this excitement was making unclear. "I ... I don't think they have a study specifically for that."

"That's what I want our project to be." The way he said it, I got the feeling there was little room for negotiation. *It's always been Andrew's way or no way. It's Andrew's game or no game at all.*

"Games, it is," I agreed.

[4]

This was how I met him. In a clumsy joining of partnership one unassuming day in Intro to Psych, we were bonded forever. The so-called questions he threw at me about how hot I thought he was, they weren't again resurrected. I was equal parts relieved and unsettled by that. Every class period thereafter, the prof would kindly give us ten minutes to discuss projects with our partners, and those ten minutes were the only ten that I began looking forward to. Even lunches and other classes and sleep got in the way; Intro to

Psych was the only thing that mattered. *Games*, he had chosen for us. *He must be into games …*

Through the course of our research, I would learn precisely how into it Andrew Knudson was. His affinity for *playing* was apparent in almost everything he did, from the intimidating way he'd stare at me knowing he'd get his way eventually, to the aggressive, almost-competitive attitude he'd take in making all the decisions with our project. I constantly felt like there was a competition going on, whether of brains or brawn I couldn't tell. The playing was endless. Once, he even bet that he could find something in the appendix quicker than I could. There were no stakes, but he'd make the bet anyway and he'd always win. Sometimes he'd be so cocky, he'd give me a head start … and *still* win. *What an expert he is with those fingers.*

When the class times apparently weren't enough to speed our progress, Andrew decided the two of us should make a workspace of my dormitory. No discussion about it, just a decision, and at once it was set in stone. *He always gets his way.* My roommate was often not there, so Andrew always sat on his bed as if he owned it. That's the way Andrew approached anything, as if it were already his to do with as he pleased. It's a quality I both admired and found furiously annoying.

When my roommate took off for a weekend, that's when the relationship between Andrew and I became something more than just a study in manipulative psychology.

"We need to be more specific," I pointed out that Friday night, scrolling through notes and bookmarked Wikipedia pages. Of course, I was the one doing all the work; he just sat there most of the time looking pretty, offering one-word responses, and only now and then bothering to crack open the textbook. "Our notes are, like, everywhere. We might as well be doing a paper on the whole field of psychology. Psychology is *all* manipulative when you think about it."

"Let's play a game."

I frowned at him. He was wearing a baby blue polo shirt. It was a size too small for his body, which gave a gift of his meaty, muscular form to my hungry eyes. Also the way he sat on my roommate's bed, it showed the crotch of his jeans in perfect view, as if taunting, deliberate. Even his *clothes* knew how to play with me. "A game?"

"We try to guess what the other's thinking."

I vividly remember feeling my heart quicken. My mouth was dry in an instant and I couldn't even swallow. Something about the way he suggested the game made me think he was already perfectly aware of the dirty thoughts crossing my quivering, ever-distracted mind. At this point, with his eyes locked onto mine and awaiting my answer, I found it excruciatingly difficult to *not* look down at the shape of his pecs in that tight baby blue polo, at the bulge his faded pants made below.

"Are you ... Are you trying to apply what we're learning about manipulative psychology to ... to ..." I tried to act all cool, tried to act casual, calm, easy.

But Andrew pressed on, ignoring me. "If you guess right, nothing happens. If you guess wrong, then you lose a piece of clothing."

"Wait, what?"

"Same applies to me. If I guess wrong, I lose a piece of clothing. *My* choice of clothing, always."

A game, he'd said. *Let's play a game.* This is how it all started. "You're really into this, huh?" I asked, but I knew I was projecting onto him because, to be honest, *I* was really into this. My cock was bone-hard in my pants to the point that it ached.

Did I really want him to see me with my clothes off? I considered that this might be a trick, a horrible prank. *He's* the one with the goods, after all. *He's* the one with the muscles and the demigod body. "How do we know we're telling the truth? I could just ... lie."

"Oh, you'll tell the truth," he said, though it sounded more like a threat. "Ready? You go first."

How far would this game go? Did we stop when we got down to our underwear? And if we were stripped naked, what would we have left to wager for every wrong answer?

My cock throbbed thinking of an answer.

"Well," I said, feeling smart, "you're obviously thinking about winning this game."

He squinted. I remember thinking, *You look so sexy when you squint. The ice in your eyes burns furious when you squint. My heart clenches with longing when you squint those fierce steely eyes.* "You sure?"

The way he asked those two words, it made me doubt everything. His voice was so powerful, his tone so persuasive, I was confident he could make me uncertain of my own name if he applied enough dominance. *He is so strong,* I knew right then. *This was a horrible mistake, to engage in a game of psychology with Andrew, the beauty from Intro.*

"Y-Yeah," I got out, annoyed at the dryness of my mouth.

Andrew grinned. I wondered if it was the first time I ever saw him smile. *It took a game to get a smile out of him.* His cheeks blushed feverishly and his eyes melted with hunger. I realized this is the way lions look when they're luring in their prey. "Correct."

I breathed a sigh of relief. "Your turn."

"You're thinking how relieved you feel," he said at once.

I couldn't argue with that. "That's cheating," I said, annoyed. "Obviously I was thinking that."

"So I'm right," he declared, the grin never leaving his face. Even his teeth shone with the saliva of a lion winning, lips wetted. "Your turn."

I shifted my legs, swallowing again despite my mouth having nothing whatsoever to swallow. "Can we get back to the paper? I'm concerned that we've spent a week or two on this and still have, like, nothing done."

"What is it?" he taunted me. "Afraid to lose your clothes?"

I steeled myself, lifting my chin. "No," I lied.

"Yeah, you are," he spat back, grinning.

"You're thinking about me losing my clothes."

Andrew's grin was gone. He snorted, annoyed. Apparently I had guessed right, because the beast in him withdrew.

"Really? I'm right?" This tickled me greatly. "Why are you, Andrew, thinking about a guy like me losing my clothes? You getting gay on me?"

"You're thinking about *me* with my clothes off," he snapped back.

"Nope." When a wash of surprise came over his fierce, sexy face, I felt myself smiling. "But now I am."

This became my goal now. He wanted to play the dorm game? We're going to play. And my goal was getting Andrew Knudson out of his tight, body-hugging clothes, watching them drop piece by piece to the floor. I wanted to see the goods he'd been hiding, the goods that only through tight fabric had I received hint of, every class long since the turn of the semester. I'd waited long enough.

He squinted at me, riled. *Oh, what those eyes can do.* Then, without being further prompted, he stood up like a good sport, unbuckled his pants, and unceremoniously threw them to his ankles. He wore sleek, black boxer-briefs that hugged his thick, muscular thighs, which were gently dusted with hair that matched the nearly-transparent blonde of his head. Plopping back down on the bed gracelessly, he kicked off the jeans along with his shoes, both of them tumbling loudly to the floor with the clinking of his heavy belt that I would someday become quite intimate with. He wore no socks. *Shoes, belt,* and *pants? Hmm. Three for one,* I thought, feeling greedy and thankful.

The boner in my pants was quite thankful too.

"What were you thinking about, then?" he asked—or rather, demanded to know.

"I was thinking about how good it'd feel to win," I told him, because it was true. "Now I know and I can move on happily with my life."

"Alright," he said, skeptical.

"What? You think I lied?"

"Yeah, I think you lied."

Perfect. My turn: "You're thinking right now about whether or not I lied."

Now it was his turn to feel cheated. "That's fucked up," he said.

"Psychology is manipulation. I take your reaction to mean I'm right."

He snorted at me. I took that for confirmation.

I felt so proud. I'd never before felt this confident in front of Andrew. And despite the look of frustration on his face, I couldn't help but notice that he seemed to be ... *enjoying* this. Something inside me had woken up, something that connected with Andrew's little dorm game. Where only a week ago Andrew had been some strange exotic and unattainable muscle boy, now we were at once speaking the same language, diving one at a time into each other's heads. *What was he about to find?*

"You're thinking about the paper again," he blurted out, thinking he'd caught me, but I shake my head, inspiring another huff of frustration from him. "What the fuck're you thinking, then?"

"How much you're enjoying this game," I said. "I was also wondering, maybe, what your p-p-pecs look like."

His eyes were sharp and cold as needles. That death-cold stare never broke from mine when, quite deliberately and slow, he rose from the bed and took hold of the bottom of his shirt. So slowly, so excruciatingly slow and careful and *slow*, he lifted the shirt, inch by inch by inch. He had my full attention. I had never wanted to see something so badly in my life. I counted his abs as the tight baby blue polo lifted, inch by inch by inch. *Oh my god*, I

breathed. *Four. Six. Eight. He has eight of them.*
Past the rolling hills of Andrew's abdomen, he
reached the mountains of pectoral muscle, the
left and the right. I was holding my breath.
Inch by inch by inch. Then his nipples peeked
out, greeting my eyes, the left and the right.
Another inch, and the curve of his two
powerful mounds of chest muscle snuck out.
The muscles in his whole torso played and
flinched and flexed as he maneuvered the tight
shirt over his thick shoulders, peeling upward,
inch by inch, up and up as he lifted his big
arms to slip the shirt off over his head. He
struggled and worked, all the while giving me
a show of his abs dancing, his pecs dancing,
wriggling as the shirt made its way off his
arms one at a time. Then, almost gently, he
flung the shirt to the bed behind him, his eyes
still on me as though they'd never broken
away, not even when the shirt was covering
them. The devil grinned in his eyes, not quite
his mouth, not *quite*, and when he licked his
lips, that's when I caught my breath.

"Your turn," said Andrew, standing there in just a pair of sleek black boxer-briefs, his voice deep and full and taunting.

"Can I just be wrong and take all my clothes off?" I half-joked, trying to make light of the fact that I was completely dressed and he was ... almost completely not.

"Rules," said Andrew, his voice booming. "You don't change the rules in the middle. You play fair, from start to end. What kind of man do you think I am?" Every word he'd say, his abdomen flexed and retracted, taking in air, then pressing it out with the words. I was so distracted by the work of art standing in front of me, I could hardly focus on what the fuck he was saying.

"I think you're an almost naked man."

"You think I'm someone who gives up?" he went on stubbornly, ignoring what I thought was a rather witty jab. "You think I'm some kid who *bends* when it's tough? The world's gonna throw shit at you, and it's gonna keep throwing shit at you. You'll be at your worst, your best friend just died, and it'll keep throwing shit. You think the world changes its rules to help you?"

"You're thinking about the world and its rules," I announced.

"The fuck right I am," he said. It didn't occur to him that I meant that as my guess, that despite his sudden bout of philosophy and life lessons, I was, in fact, still playing the game. "The world is fucked up when we come into it, it's fucked up when we go. Nothing changes that."

He looked so beautiful standing there, almost yelling at me, his muscles flexing and unflexing with all his speech and passion and fervor.

"You get me?"

I looked up to meet his eyes. I saw the zeal in them. He was having fun a moment ago, but now he was made furious at the mere suggestion of me breaking the game, forfeiting, or otherwise tampering with his apparently-set-into-stone-like-law rules that he'd made. *He takes this shit seriously,* I realized, attempting to sober myself. *He takes this shit really, really seriously. This is not just a game.*

"I get you," I said, though it came out in more of a meek, dry choke. *Was I ever going to kiss his lips? Can he make my fantasies realized, and suddenly express that all this gaming and playing around and teasing and taunting is, in fact, just his version of foreplay, and that we were about to crash faces as soon as he could get my clothes off?*

"So you stick to the fucking rules," he said.

"Got it."

"No dicking around. No second tries or mistakes. If you don't respect the rules, you respect nothing. If you don't learn discipline, you don't learn anything."

"Got it." Discipline. *Discipline. Do you want to discipline me, Andrew?*

"Now make your guess," he ordered me.

I smiled. "I already had. And I got it right." When his eyebrows pulled together, quizzical, I watched it slowly dawn on him. I remember thinking: *He has such a beautiful face, he has to be a model or at the very least part-god.* "Your turn."

His jaw locked, set and gnawing on his own teeth. He knew he only had one more wrong answer before he was completely naked. I knew he only had one more wrong answer before he was completely naked. I was certain that, no matter what he said, I'd tell him he was wrong. I'd tell him just so I could have him banish away that final scrap of fabric on his sexy body. I'd lie to him just to watch him remove his last piece of dignity. *Dignity never looked so sexy. Heaven's never been so close to me, within reach, within touch ... Just one wrong answer away.*

He said, "You're thinking I only have one wrong answer left before losing." His eyes burned with the fury of a million games he'd played in the past, a million more he'll play in the future. His chest, puffed with confidence. He's a man who always wins, a man who gets his way, a champion, a competitor.

With every article of clothing that Andrew lost, my confidence grew twofold. I found myself licking my lips. *You're thinking I only have one wrong answer left before losing,* he'd said.

Right, I thought. "Wrong," I breathed instead.

He showed no reaction; his eyes simply continued to burn me whole. Then, after too long a time, he asked, "Then what is it you're thinking?"

"How big your cock is, and whether or not it can fit in my mouth."

He took a step toward me. He took another step, his heavy bare feet slapping the dorm room floor. Another. Then he stood right in front of me. My legs apart, he stood between them, invading my space, his face baring down on me and the crotch of his tight boxer-briefs *right there*, enveloping my blurry, quivery field of vision.

Then his fingers found the waistband, slipping underneath. I broke from his eyes to stare ahead at the show of his clever fingers. The waistband dropped half an inch, the fabric bunching up, the *sound* of the fabric alone enticing me, lifting all the hairs on the back of my neck. The *sound* of the fabric as it slipped another half inch, revealing two cut hips, slowly unveiling the "V" of muscle that led to his cock. The boxer-briefs held back little from the imagination; I was already plenty aware how big he was.

Until even this moment, Andrew had *never* indicated one way or another his sexual interests. He'd never ogled a woman *or* a guy in my presence. Not once did he make mention of a girlfriend, of a boyfriend, of a chick he found hot or a dude he'd want to slam. His sexual appetite was a complete and agonizing mystery to me. Until this moment when his crotch was literally two-and-a-half inches from my face, I'd never even had the gall to give it an honest wonder. It's so strange, how a person can just *be* sexuality ... how a person could make you forget heterosexuality, homosexuality, anything that limits or defines or categorizes ... that Andrew was, somehow, inexplicably, unexplainably just ... there for the meal.

Yes, the fabric was still slipping off. I saw the hint of hair peeking out. *He manscapes*, I thought, and it amused me, almost inspiring a smile. *He cares*, I realized it meant. *He's a groomer.* The base of his cock was next to reveal itself, the underwear coming slowly, slowly, slowly off. He makes a game out of everything, knowing how bad I want it. I had half a mind to make a grab at his boxers, to yank them off and claim my prize, but something held me back.

I didn't really earn this, I realized, a tinge of guilt working its way into my somersaulting cocktail of excitement and horniness happening downstairs. *I won the sight of his cock with a lie. I cheated. I broke the rule ... arguably, the only rule of the game.*

When he pulled the rest of his boxers down, sliding them slowly over the hills of his upper thighs, his cock slapped me in the face, and I didn't care anymore how I'd earned the win, from deceit or otherwise. His cock remained there, pointing out, pressing itself against my cheek like a friend who's come at me for a hug.

The boxers laid at his ankles, and when I peered up, I found Andrew still staring down at me mightily, like some giant beast. Even his pecs seemed to stare at me, his nipples punctuating the peak of either mountain of muscle. To my immediate right, his cock still graced my cheek.

Was he expecting something? No more words came from him. I wondered if this meant the game was over, now that he'd lost all his clothes. His cock against my face, it neither flexed nor flinched nor pulsed; it merely waited there, strong, powerful and keen.

I took this for an invitation. What the fuck else was it meant to be? I parted my lips, began to turn my cheek.

"No," he barked from the top of the mountain.

I stopped, lips still parted, his cock literally a centimeter from entering them. My eyes stared up at him like some puppy from the floor. *No?* I could feel myself wanting to whimper like a puppy too. *No?* But his cock was right there. His cock was waiting, wasn't it? Wasn't he?

"If you want to suck me off," he said finally, "then you gotta get the next question right."

The disbelief poured out of my eyes. My lips were still parted, I was still frozen in place with his cock—*my prize*—resting gently in the air before my mouth, and I choked: "A-An-Another game?"

"Yes."

"Haven't we played enough?"

"A simple game. One question. You get it right, you get my cock. You get it wrong, I leave and you don't see me until class Monday."

WHAT?? I pulled away right then, staring up at him exasperatedly, my jaw hanging. *What the fuck was he getting out of this?* "Dude," I argued, feeling incensed, "it's *your* cock that's getting the blowjob. It's a reward for us both, isn't it? Why do we have to make another fucking game out of it? I don't understand."

"You playing, or am I going?"

He was having none of my protests, nor my questions, nor my appeal to simple logic. Didn't he *want* me to suck him off? Or does every sexual action between us have to be motivated with the winning or losing of a game?

Well, I started the day not knowing what Andrew's naked body looked like. Now I knew, so whether a blowjob happened or not, I'm not leaving the day empty-handed. Nothing here to lose, really, only something to gain.

In my mouth.

So I finally asked: "What's the question?"

He reached down suddenly, wrapped his

cock with his mighty hand, pressed it against the side of my face and asked: "How many inches is it?"

Are you kidding me? His cock was right there, pressed against my face, and there was no way I could possibly see it, no way I could possibly guess. The only moment I'd had of judging its entirety was a split-second after the boxer-briefs went down before the man-monster slapped me in the cheek. *So fucking cruel,* I thought, *to have the answer pressed into my cheek where I can't see it.* It could've been nine inches. Could've been eight. Hell, having only seen it within centimeters of my face, it might've been four inches and simply *looked* enormous so close-up. How the fuck could I know for sure? Was it hard, or is he more of a grower than a shower?

He must be thinking of the answer right now. Andrew must be thinking of it, and this is almost like just another round of our previous game. *What number are you thinking of? How many inches is little Andrew?* Difference is, the stakes in this particular question were considerably higher.

"Seven," I answered.

Andrew didn't move for a moment. His firm fist still obnoxiously pressing his cock into my cheek, I heard him murmur: "You sure?"

He wants you to be right, I told myself. *He wants a blowjob—Who wouldn't? He's trying to help you.*

"Eight," I said, changing my mind.

The cock still pressed to my face, torturing me, driving me crazy, Andrew murmured once again: "You sure?"

Those two cruel fucking words. Those two evil, horrible motherfucking words.

"Eight and a half," I choked. "Nine."

Then Andrew pulled away. I felt a stab of excitement until suddenly I realized he was pulling up his underwear. I didn't even think to look at his cock until it was already put away. Then he began slipping a foot each into his pants.

"Andrew," I said.

He pulled the pants up, yanked them over his thighs, did the buckle loudly. The whole time he dressed, his eyes never left my face. He took up the polo shirt from the bed, slipped it over his head, working his way into the arms. There went his pecs I was so craving, there went his abs, there went his sexy bellybutton.

"Andrew?"

He reached down and pulled on his shoes, slowly doing the laces, taking his time.

"You're not seriously leaving?" I blurted, all the fun dropping from me in an instant. "Andrew?"

That's when the wicked grin spread across his face. Pulling the backpack over his shoulder, he didn't say another word and, unhurriedly, he went to the door.

"Andrew, seriously?"

The door shut softly behind him. I stumbled to my feet, pulled open the door and stared after him as he walked down the hall.

"What the fuck!" I called out.

He disappeared into the stairwell, the heavy door shutting behind him. I was left alone, standing at my dorm room with my cock throbbing in my pants.

I'd won the game, yet left a loser.

[5]

Had I done something wrong? Had I said something? I hardly said anything. Half of me wanted to run after him, but I can't imagine myself acting so desperate. Was the whole thing a ploy to fuck with my head? Maybe he'd been listening more than I thought he had during all our research on manipulative psychology. Maybe this whole diabolical cock-torture was his plan from the start. Talk about applying what you learn. Fuck.

The rest of Friday night I spent sulking in front of the TV, watching a rerun of some bullshit something. I didn't even eat dinner so my stomach sang sweet grumbly songs of misery all night to match the drumming of my heart. Saturday went much the same. I kept my cellphone close, as if he'd call or text or something. We had each other's numbers. I ate in the dorm cafeteria for lunch *and* dinner that day, thinking there was some small, stupid chance he'd still be around and I'd catch him. I didn't even know where he lived, whether in another dorm on campus, or off-campus in some fraternity-riddled subdivision or maybe he even had his own apartment. For all I knew, these dumb little efforts at trying to run into him on a weekend would prove fruitless.

Saturday night I jerked off. I don't even remember the porn I watched. Sunday was no different, though it was filled with remarkably less hope. *How the fuck am I going to face him Monday?* That was the question I couldn't stop asking myself. *I've seen him naked,* I kept thinking, over and over. *I've seen Andrew*

Knudson naked and his cock, his cock, his cock was pressed against my face.

My cheek was more intimate with Andrew's cock than my mouth was, and that made no sense to me whatsoever.

Monday hit me like a storm and I worried in the morning I'd not have the balls to go to class. When I finally coaxed myself into some clothes and heaved my heavy textbook-filled backpack over a shoulder, I trekked across campus to the psychology building. Every step threatened to buckle my knees. Pushing open the door to the psychology building made me lose my breath. When I reached the door to the classroom, I had to stop and shut my eyes. My face was on fire, I could feel it. *I don't think I can do this,* I realized, trembling and wanting to cry.

Then I pushed into the room and, without paying mind to anything or anyone else in the class, I blindly stumbled to my seat. There I remained, breathing slowly and horribly, counting imaginary minutes until the class would be over.

The professor began to talk and if a million dollars were laid down I still couldn't tell you what the hell today's lesson covered. Twice, only twice, I looked up from my hands and brought my eyes to his desk—to *Andrew's* desk. He sat facing forward, a striped blue and white shirt hugging his body. I couldn't even quiver with excitement at the sight of him; I was much too scared, too anxious, too worried of things that had happened, of things that hadn't happened. *Look back at me*, I begged, but he didn't so much as flinch. Only twice I looked.

At ten minutes left, the professor released us to discussing the project with our partners. For the third time, I looked up, but only Andrew's backside greeted me.

I took a deep, deep, deep breath. It was a jagged breath, but it gave me the strength to rise to my feet. I clumsily put one foot in front of the other, brought myself to the side of Andrew's desk.

Then, he turned to look at me. His grey-blue eyes seemed lazy, almost tired. "Hey," he said.

I lowered myself into the seat next to him and said nothing for a while, trembling. He lifted his eyebrows expectantly.

"You look sick," he said.

I opened my mouth, closed it, then opened it again to speak. "Are we okay? You and I?"

"Yeah." He shrugged. "Why wouldn't we be?"

I felt my breath become more even. I felt my chest relax. My fingertips were tingly and icy cold, all the blood having retreated from my limbs, apparently. "I just, uh ..." How the fuck would I put it into words? "After I ... I lost the game, I ..."

"This your way of saying you want to do another one?" His voice was almost gentle.

No, I didn't want any games. *I just want to know what your cock feels like inside me. In my mouth. In my body. I want to give you a reason to lose all your cool, to drop the stoicism and the hardness and adopt, instead, another hardness below your waist. I want to give you reason to moan like a bitch and cry out so loud all my hallmates hear and wonder whose buck is getting banged. I want to get you and your beefcake body naked again without the permission of another fucking game.*

"Yes," I said instead.

[6]

The second time my roommate went out of town for the weekend, Andrew took the chance and declared my dorm as our study hall. Also, our paper was kinda fucking due the following Monday and we'd written precisely zero percent of it.

"I'm not a good writer," he complained, seated in the chair at my roommate's desk.

The laptop was growing hot on my thighs where I typed, seated cross-legged on the bed. "You don't have to be. I'm typing it out, you just need to help me think."

"I'm not a good thinker."

"I have a thesis figured out. Kinda. I have our notes here. I know what we're going to say, just ... I need a little more input from you, Andrew."

"I'm the inspiration." He folded his arms, spinning around in my roommate's swivel chair. I got the pleasure of watching his body in three hundred and sixty degrees as it rotated. He wore a plain white t-shirt with a pair of torn jeans today. "Without me, the paper would be boring. Hey." He stopped spinning, facing me. "Let's play."

"Let's write." I typed out the intro paragraph, worked a thesis into it somehow. Of course, my mind kept warring with me. One side hollered at me to pay mind to the deliciously big boy sitting in the chair. The other side panicked for the soon-approaching deadline. Then there's the issue of how my cock kept throbbing gallingly at me every five seconds. It was like I could still feel Andrew's cock pressed against my cheek. *He looks really good in that shirt,* I reasoned, then realized he'd look good in any shirt he wore. What a stupid thing to think.

I bit my lip, frustrated beyond all hell, then finally met Andrew's hungry eyes with my own. "Before we play again, I want to make a new rule."

"Fine. New rule is—"

"New rule is," I took over, not allowing the ever-bossy Andrew to take charge as he always does, "no consequence of any game is you *leaving* the dorm and not coming back all weekend. That's just stupid, and if you're not going to help me with this paper, then we both fail. Got it?"

He stood up from the chair at once and rushed to the bed. I only had time to let out a gasp before my laptop was flung to the side and Andrew Knudson sat on me. His hands pinned mine above my head to the wall and he was straddling my lap, his power-thighs trapping me. His face, stern and iron-cold, stayed a mere two inches from mine. I could feel his every breath on my face.

"The rule," he said in a voice so low it crept up my spine and tickled the little hairs in my ear, "is that you gotta stay absolutely fucking still."

"Okay."

"And no talking."

I nodded.

My hands were still pinned to the wall behind me. He kept them there with just one of his hands. *He's so strong.* The other hand traced down my arm, slowly, like a drop of water or a tiny bug. I flinched a bit when he approached my underarm.

"Stay still," he said, and his voice carried a lilt of warning. "That's the only rule. Stay still or you lose."

"But it—!"

"And no talking. Wasn't I clear?" His face inches from mine, I felt myself breathing hard and heavy. My cock was so hard, I felt like I was leaking bad. I clenched shut my lips, clamped, tight, clenching and clenching.

His hand began to move again.

When he got to my underarm, it was almost unbearable. I shivered and shivered, trying with all my nerves not to squirm and laugh. *Is this the point of the game?* I wondered. *Is this a tickling game?* The slower his hand moved across my armpit, the harder I got. The sensations were driving me wild. I felt a pox of goose bumps all over my body. He had my hands pinned high above me, but he even had my legs pinned too, held firmly beneath the weight of his own body. I was all his to do with as he pleased ... and it seemed he pleased to do a lot.

"Doing good," he said, as if it helped ease the torment of sensations wriggling through my growing-ever-the-more-sensitive body.

"How long's this last??"

"Until you fuck up," he answered. "Shut up."

His hand continued down to my chest. I almost squeaked when his wicked fingers reached my right nipple. *Oh my god.* He lingered there quite deliberately; he must've noticed something in my face, whether it was a flinch or a squirm of an eyebrow. He began to tease my nipple, slowly, gently. Then he pinched it. I shut my eyes and bit my lip. *Fuck being tickled,* I thought. *This feels good.*

But then his evil hand slid to my side, and before I knew it he'd entered the next most-sensitive area imaginable: my ribs. I took in a deep and futile breath as his hand played devilishly down my side. It wasn't so bad until his fingers started to move, like five individual ticklers, each with a mind worse than the next. *He knows what he's doing,* I knew. *He's an expert.* He was so gentle, so, so gentle. Not to mention, I also still had the problem of a certain throbbing *something* between my legs that couldn't be tamed.

"You won my pants," he announced. I opened my eyes, lifted my brow. Is it safe to talk? "Keep it up longer and you get my shirt."

No fucking way. The longer I last, the more naked he'll get? I felt a smile break across my face.

Andrew, notably *not* smiling, leaned in as his hand began to move again. "Yeah, sounds nice and all. But the game ends when your silence does."

With that, I felt his fingers go lower. Lower. Lower. Before I realized what he was doing, his mischievous grin had returned and my mouth flung open in a silent gasp. He tugged once, and the button to my pants flew off. He tugged again and a zipper slid down. My eyes grew double.

"Moaning counts," he muttered. And then his hand gripped my swollen cock. My jaw dropped further to emit a yelp of surprise, a gasp, a groan, *something*, but nothing emerged but silence and nothing and *nothing*. His fingers, now the five little masters of my cock, began stroking.

This was no tickle torment anymore. Shit just got serious.

He neither moved nor spoke for a while. My legs were trapped and useless beneath his body, and my hands were still pinned to the wall. I had nowhere to go, nowhere to hide, nowhere to look but right into his delicious, horrible face. His own lips parted. He was excited; this was his *thing*. I could see the hunger in his eyes, the yearning, the longing ... but perhaps it was more the hunger for winning that I was seeing, not something else.

His jerking of my cock quickened. "Don't even think about moaning," he threatened. I felt my toes curling; at least he couldn't see *them*. I'd let all my excitement out through the expressive wringing and wriggling and curling and uncurling of my toes, but never in my body. *I have to win*, I realized. *I have to get his shirt off again.* Ever since that cruel Friday, I'd hungered so bad to see him shirtless. I wanted his body and I would pay almost any price.

I was getting close. He's an expert jerker of the male member. My breathing was quick, but even *that* had to be quieted in order to win. I couldn't make a sound, not even the rasping of breath. It was a silence nearly impossible to maintain.

But all the restraint of physical expression only made me that much more aware of my sense of touch. The way he worked my cock, if only I had the freedom of voice, I'd be squealing and yelping and moaning and clawing at him.

I felt my cock pulsing, pulsing, reaching the point of no return. My eyes began to rock back.

"Oh god," I blurted out.

And just as he let go, my cock erupted. *Don't stop*, I wanted to scream, agonized, frustrated, but it was too late, and with my eyes clamped shut, I felt wave after wave of cum thrusting out of me. I cried out, moaned, and my wrists fought against his powerful hand, squirming, my legs and thighs wrestling under the weight of his body.

My eyes shot open and I kept yanking on my hands, desperate to continue jerking myself. "Why'd you fucking stop??" I exclaimed, out of breath, my cock dribbling now, bobbing up and down, as desperate as the jagged breath I'm trying to catch.

"You made a sound," he said simply. "You lost."

I inhaled three times, filling my lungs, trying so feebly to calm myself. Then finally I shouted, "Is that what this is about?? You won't—" I took a breath, let it out, "—do anything sexual with another dude unless the rules of some game—" I took a breath, let it out, "—allow you to?"

He didn't address my question. He only glanced down at his chest, then frowned. "You got jizz on my shirt."

"Maybe that's what our paper should've been about," I breathed, feeling my pulse in my throat. "Denial. Got a whole chapter on that, I'm pretty sure. Maybe its own textbook, even."

"No one's denying anything," he said finally, meeting my eyes. "I like games. It's what gets me off. And also, I'm a man of my word."

Finally he let go, slid off the bed, and began to unbuckle his pants. I brought down my arms to nurse two sore, tingling wrists and watched as Andrew threw aside his belt like a bothersome thing and popped his own pants open. With a thrust, he dropped them to his ankles and stood proud. Today, he wore a loose pair of blue and green plaid boxers. They did not hide his own cock well.

"So you've made a mess of me all over my bed," I point out. "Is this my reward? Getting to see your legs?"

He shrugged. "I'll pull them back up if you're not interested." Even as he said it, he bent down to retrieve his fallen pants.

"No," I blurted out. He stopped, lifting a brow at me. "Don't you dare. The sight of your legs is my ... my prize and ... I want it."

"More than finishing a psychology paper?"

"We'll get to that later. Right now, I want to enjoy what a bunch of unnecessary tickling and a nipple-pinching and half an interrupted cum just earned me."

"Either this or the paper." He crossed his arms, looking like some muscle beast, waiting.

"Huh?" I pulled myself to the edge of the bed, minding the cum that was turning cold on my still-exposed and softening cock. "How's that a fair choice? We *have* to do the paper. It's due Monday. We've had four weeks now."

"Paper or me."

"That's bullshit." I couldn't believe he was making me choose. It just wasn't reasonable at all. Like picking whether to eat or breathe for a day and only being able to choose one.

"What's your answer?"

"Don't you care about your own grade? If we don't do the paper—"

"Either we work on the paper," he spoke, obnoxiously slow, as if I was the dumb kid in the back of the class with the drool hanging from my slack mouth, "or I keep my pants off. One or the other. You can't have both."

"What is this?" I asked, challenging him. "*Another* fucking game?"

"Make your choice, boy."

Boy.

Boy ...

This was the first time he ever called me boy. With that one word, he put me in my place, from then on. That one word branded me, collared me. I didn't quite realize it then, but from that point until now, I would be his boy ... his toy ... his glad and willing game-thing.

And what kind of boy, exactly, did that make me? What kind of boy did that make him?

"Fuck the paper," I breathed.

[7]

Two trying weeks later, I would discover that Andrew and I had made a C- on our paper. More accurately, *I* had made a C- on our paper, as I was its only author. It was the first C- I'd ever made in my entire life. High school showered me in A's and B's. Every other class, I saw A's and B's, and when I saw that C- on the paper, I felt a stab of joy.

Yes, a stab of joy. That C- was my freedom. That C- was my permission to let the fuck go, to relax, to slay the demon of perfection that had so haunted my adolescence. "C fucking minus," I said, reading the grade aloud. Some guy next to me gave me a sympathetic frown, leaned in and said, "Sorry, dude. Better luck next time." His face turned queer when the smile of pride washed over my face, beaming positively at the C- and the world that'd been opened before me and everything that stupid, shitty grade meant.

But with the ending of the psychology project, Andrew and I no longer had a reason to meet. Not that the paper was ever fully our focus. But I could not let us drift apart, not after what had been so suddenly and hotly birthed between our warring, playful minds.

"Hey, Andy," I called out, chasing after him through the doors when class had ended.

Without turning around, I heard him grunt, "Don't call me that."

I had caught up to him, walking beside him on the road between the psych hall and the architecture building. "Where you off to?"

"Algebra."

"Want to grab lunch after?"

"No."

I was reaching here. Totally fucking desperate. That psych paper couldn't be the only thing that brought us together. There had to be something more. "So what're you doing after Algebra, then?"

"Going home."

"Do you live on campus?"

"No."

"Do you want to?"

"Maybe."

"Why don't you want to grab some lunch before you leave, then?"

"I'll get it on my own."

I stood in front of him, exasperated. I couldn't let this dream slip away from me so easily. "What the fuck, Andrew?"

He walked around me, not daunted in the least by my sad attempt at trying to stop him. He just kept going, sauntering down the path without paying me a cent of mind. He was near the door to the algebra building. I had to act fast.

"How about a deal then?" I shouted at his back as he reached the door. "If your Algebra class is totally lame as fuck, then I win, and you gotta come to my dorm afterwards for lunch."

To that, he turned his head, gave me a big grin, then flicked me off as he disappeared into the math building. I took that to mean the deal was accepted.

An hour later, he knocked on my dorm room door. "Lame as fuck," he agreed when I answered.

And so it began. For weeks, we expertly snuck around my roommate's schedule—which blissfully consisted of a lot of trips back home, weekends spent with the girlfriend or the parents, and days where he just wanted to stay out all night in town—and Andrew and I played and played and played. Whenever he arrived at my door, I knew it was time for our next dorm game.

One time, he had me tied up with an elastic band he used to work out and do stretches, then proceeded to ask me questions about himself, like his birthday, or his favorite TV show, or even the color of the socks he was wearing. "What color underwear do I got on?" he asked once, and the agony of knowing that the answer was hidden right in front of me beneath the sexy fold of denim at his crotch was unbearable. "You're hard," he observed. Tied up, there was little I could do to hide it. Every right answer earned me a piece of his clothing coming off. Every wrong answer earned me a piece of his clothing going back on. If I could get him naked in ten questions or less, I'd get his cock in my mouth. "This is killing me," I complained, so horny and frustrated, but he only licked his lips, half-dressed, and asked the next question.

I didn't get to suck his cock. Somehow I knew he'd planned it from the start, as it was upon the eleventh question that I finally earned his naked body, but no cock play.

A normal person would've given up on him by now. I'd decided that I was, without a doubt, far from normal.

Later in the year, he thought it'd be an amazing idea to belittle me with his strength by engaging in some more ... *physical* games. One such game involved us holding a weight in either hand, requiring us to keep them elevated at shoulder height. To win, I, with my puny muscles, had to hold up a weight longer than him, the demigod. I knew he was at an unfair advantage and I didn't care. Something about the experience of suffering near him, sweating, struggling, feeling my muscles cramping and aching while he stood there, perfectly at ease, cocky, a triumphant smirk on his face the whole time, made me so hard that I could've cum right there.

After we'd play and have ourselves declared a winner and a loser, he would seem to grow restless, unsure of what to do, then eventually decide to go. I'd always have to make sure we had our next game planned, just so I'd be assured that I would see Andrew again. Whenever he left, my heart felt heavy and the world grew small and cold. Lying there on the bed, I'd hardly acknowledge my roommate when he'd return at two in the morning and rush to the shower. *Good for him,* I remember thinking. *At least my roommate's getting some action. I've been mindfucked all semester by Andrew and yet haven't fucked or been fucked at all.*

What a cruel concept, to have so much sexless sex with someone. We were so strangely intimate, and yet hadn't been intimate at all.

That needed to change. And soon.

Even this late in the game, I still couldn't say with confidence whether Andrew was gay or straight or experimental or something else entirely. He seemed to have little interest in sex. I couldn't even say whether he found me attractive. I was, by no means, a super sexy guy. *Andrew* was a super sexy guy. The only thing that seemed to keep his interest at all were these weird, sexually-frustrated, mind-fucky sort of power games. Sure, I found them erotic. I usually had a stiffy from start to end, but there was something emotionally *missing* for me. Was it missing for him, too?

For one, he never kissed. I've wanted to put my lips to his so badly that I've dreamt it several nights in a row. Also, he never allowed us to do anything incredibly intimate unless it was within the context of a game. With my somewhat limited psych knowledge, I considered whether this was a form of denial or not. It almost reminded me of the type of guy that would only do gay things if he was super, super drunk or stoned. It's like he could just blame the drug—or the game—for making him do shit with a guy. It somehow made it ... acceptable.

There had to be something else in him. There had to be something more in him than just these fucking games. Where was his soul? Where was his passion and his gallantry and his humor?

I needed to figure it out. I refused to believe it didn't exist. It's time to manifest my own power. It's time to bring the player to a different table.

It was time to play *my* game.

[8]

One innocent Tuesday, there was the expected knock at my door, right on cue. I opened it without acknowledging the scrumptious Andrew, then sat myself on the bed and returned to watching TV. Some lame show was on and I gave it all my fake attention. Seeing me all chilled out, the remote balanced on my belly, he lazily threw himself into my roommate's desk chair, kicked up his feet, and let out a long, obnoxious yawn. For the next ten minutes, neither of us said a thing, allowing the murmur from the TV to do all the talking.

"Bet I could—" he started to say.

"Bet you could too," I interrupted, letting out a small yawn of my own. "Hey, do you know what we're watching?"

Andrew squinted at the screen. "No. I don't really watch TV."

"Neither do I."

The TV kept spilling its mud mess of colors over our faces, the sun through the window nearly set for the day. Andrew finally had an instinct to turn on the desk lamp, I guess to save us from the swallowing darkness of the night. We were coming up on the half-hour and one stupid TV sitcom was traded for the next. Every time Andrew glanced over at me, I made sure my eyes were glued to the TV.

My little trick worked, though it took so awful long to know that it had. "Wanna do something?"

"I'd kinda like to just chill," I answered. "Ever since my workout this afternoon, I've had a bad cramp in my calf. Kinda making me miserable."

"Hmm." He stared at my leg, uncertain.

"It sucks," I said, hoping my *prompting* him isn't too obvious.

Then, he took the bait. "Which leg?"

"My right. The calf."

"Lie back," he said. I lifted a nonchalant brow at him. "Go ahead, lie back. On your stomach."

I sprawled out on the bed, pressed my face into the pillow and waited. I listened to him rise from the desk chair, then felt the bed compress as he sat on it. His hands embraced my leg, and I felt him slowly begin to rub it. The instant he touched me, I was hard as steel.

"Thirsty?" I asked.

I heard him grunt, then ask, "Why?"

"My roommate has beer in the fridge."

For a moment, I worried he was about to whine that he doesn't drink. To my surprise, my *second* bit of bait was taken, and I listened to him reaching for the fridge—which was conveniently at the foot of my bed—and the tiny door opened, a can was fetched, and the tiny door shut with a gentle *thump*. He cracked open the can, and I heard him chugging. I felt a strange giddiness tickling up my body, listening to him drink my roommate's illegal beer. If he was ever caught with it ...

"I'm getting another," he said when he was done. "Want one?"

"Nah. Have as many as you like." As if I needed to give him permission; we both knew Andrew would help himself to as many beers as he damn well pleased.

A whole six-pack of empty and crushed beer cans on my floor later, he was back to running his hands down my "cramped" leg. Yeah, it wasn't cramped at all, the whole thing was a sneaky, sexy lie, but tonight I was insisting on our playing *my* game. He didn't have to be aware he was playing. He was so used to his own form of denials; what's the harm in introducing him to another?

"You should feel more relaxed now."

"Yes." I shut my eyes and breathed into the pillow. His hands climbed and climbed, working my calf muscle into a state of blissful, melted butter. I wanted to bite the pillow. I think I might have, clawing the sheets. I knew he had skillful hands and yet I still wasn't prepared for the gourmet-caliber massage I was getting.

"It'll hurt a bit," he warned me. "In a good way." His thumbs went deep into my calf, pressing and kneading and pressing and *pressing*. I moaned a bit, squirming. It definitely hurt, but with his firm grasp on my leg, I surely wasn't going anywhere. How does he make every gift—even a massage—feel like something I have to earn through suffering or endurance of some kind?

"Thanks," I choked out, trying not to pull my leg away.

"Don't thank me yet."

His hands moved up my leg, began to work my lower thigh. I couldn't believe how much power lived in just his fingertips, how he could make such an impression on me through the thick material of my jeans. *It's like I'm not even wearing them,* I thought—which led me to an even tastier thought.

"Should I take my jeans off?" I asked. "I mean, would it make it ... I don't know ... easier?"

"Not really," he said.

I spun around, got to my feet anyway. He let me, looking up to meet my eyes with his watery ones. *He's buzzed*, I realized. *Good. Right where I want you.* I undid my pants, let them drop to the floor. They landed with an unimpressive thump on the carpet.

Without any shoes or socks to kick off, I simply stepped out of them and hopped back onto my bed, putting my leg in his lap. "Go ahead," I told him, like an order. "Right where you left off."

He gripped my leg, but his hands were tender this time ... careful and deliberate. He still kneaded my calf muscle firmly, but something about him changed. *Is my plan working?* I wondered, hopeful. *Was I breaking through his walls? Had I found the fissure in his otherwise impenetrable armor?*

"The year is almost over," I pointed out as his fingers worked up my calf again, reaching my lower thigh, massaging and rubbing.

"Finals are on us," he agreed, his words subtly slurring together. "Might, dunno, need your help in studying or something."

"I could help. You'll have to help me too." I kept shut my eyes, enjoying his hand as it worked up my lower thigh ... up, higher, higher. "I was also wondering if, like, y'know, if you'd given any thought to your, uh, your living arrangements or whatever." It was a bit awful to be the sober one in the room. Too much thought was happening in my head. Too many fears that beer might have otherwise quieted. Maybe I should've downed one or two to make it all a bit less—whatever it was.

"What do you mean?"

"Where you're planning to live next year," I clarified. "My roommate might be moving out. And I don't want them to stick some random other dude in here, y'know. I'd kinda prefer, well ..."

"Someone you know," he finished for me.

Oh my god, was he already considering it? Was he considering it before? He was on my same train of thought; I could tell from the way he ended my sentence. "Yeah?" I prompted him, feeling my heart rate accelerate. Just the thought of having him around all the time made me suffocate with excitement. "You've given it some thought, then?"

"Could work out," he reasoned, his hands still moving up, up, up, creeping like an ambush of ten horny boys, each a fingertip, up the terrain of my leg. Soon, he'd run out of thigh to massage. *Where are those wicked hands headed next?*

This was my game. He didn't know it, but he was playing my game now and I was in control.

Quite suddenly, I flipped over onto my

back, placing my leg into his lap again, this time facing up and watching his eyes carefully. He squinted quizzically at me, his blue-grey irises shining.

"Front side now," I said. "The cramp's moved up my thigh."

"Alright." He started massaging it, his watery eyes not leaving my face, full of skepticism and suspicion. But his gaze was also clouded by the alcohol, making his suspicion appear more like confusion. *I couldn't have planned this better ...*

In my underwear, face-up, I couldn't hide the erection his steadily-kneading palms and fingertips gave me. He knew it. I knew it. The both of us were obviously aware of the big tent in my loose plaid boxers. Still, he struggled to keep his intense, watery stare on me, blinking away the buzz of the beer that threatened to loosen him too far. I kept my innocent eyes on his, studying him almost curiously as he smoothly worked my leg with the concentration of a steelworker.

He reached the upper part of my thigh now ... and I felt his fingertips grazing the rim of my underwear. If he kept moving up my leg, his hands would slip effortlessly under my boxers. Just the thought made my cock bob. His fingers kept tickling my underwear, barely disrupting the fabric just enough for my cock to become agonizingly aware of it.

And then my hard-as-fuck cock slipped through the fly, poking out in all its bareness, greeting the world. Andrew's eyes went to it right away, almost as though he were startled. My cock pointed to the sky, bobbing in sync with the thrashing heart in my chest, with the pumping of my excited veins and the pulse of my life.

Our eyes didn't meet again. He was transfixed on the new attendee of our massage party. His hands had become distracted then, hardly paying attention to the massage, losing all their drive. *Wow*, I wondered. *I didn't realize my cock demanded such attention.*

He parted his lips suddenly, brought his

mouth upon my cock, and it was gone, swallowed whole by Andrew Knudson on my dorm room bed.

I threw my head back with a rasp of surprise. My hands instinctively went to his soft head of hair. My throat formed a howl that I never released and I couldn't close my mouth, jagged of breath and stiff as stone.

His mouth moved up and down my cock, up and down and up. His hands suddenly found a purpose, gripping my hips at either side. My fingers still played in his hair, feeling his head as it went up and down and up again.

When finally I felt his tongue begin to join the party, a groan wrested its way out of my chest.

My legs had nowhere to go, once again trapped under Andrew's muscled weight. All this time, I was certain I'd be the first one to taste his cock, and not the other way around.

He didn't seem to have a desire to stop, either. The sucking went on and on. It drove me so crazy I had a sudden fear that I'd erupt in his mouth. I wondered if he'd like that or if it'd destroy the moment—whatever the fuck this moment was that we were having.

His hands rushed up my body suddenly, slipping under my shirt and making a dance across my bare belly and chest. As if finding home, his fingers arrived at each of my nipples, and my left nipple made a friend with his evil left hand, my right nipple with his evil right.

"Oh god," I blurted out as he pinched my nipples too hard—that is, exactly hard enough. I squirmed underneath him, but he didn't budge an inch, still working his hoover of a mouth on my throbbing cock. "Ooh god, ooh god," I started saying over and over. It was like I had no choice; I had to exclaim what his fingers and his mouth were doing to me.

And this was no game anymore. This was two normal boys messing around in a dorm room. This was the culmination of something *real*, yes ... that's what this was. Something natural that came about totally ... organically.

Yes, something that I didn't need to coax him for months to do, something that I didn't need the aid of six cans of beer and a teasing massage to get him to do. Right.

Fuck it. I didn't care. I had my fingers in Andrew Knudson's hair and my cock between his plush, dexterous lips and his tongue working miracles. In my game, there were no losers.

Suddenly he came up from my cock, his mouth wetted by his efforts, and he started undoing his own pants. *Oh my god, is this about to happen?* That's what I thought as I sat up to watch Andrew struggle with his belt, nearly tear it off, then kick his pants off. Climbing back onto the bed, he pulled out his own cock from over the waistband of his sexy tight boxer-briefs and began to jerk off in front of me. I stared, gawking.

"Eight inches," I decided, staring as he jerked off while straddling my legs, the tips of our cocks so close they could kiss. "Definitely eight."

"Seven." He squinted down at me. "Objects in mirror are bigger than they appear." We both bust out laughing for a split-second, then went right back to our ever-serious staring at one another.

"Can I jerk off with you?" I asked quietly.

It felt stupid to ask, as if I needed to request permission to touch myself, but something told me that's exactly what Andrew would like to hear.

At my question, he suddenly grabbed my cock with his other hand and began to stroke. I gasped, taken anew by the wild sensations he made chase through my body. Both our cocks in his control, he jerked and jerked and jerked.

"Here's the deal," he said, his voice still bent a touch to the left with his slurring. "Whoever cums first loses."

No. No games. "How about we just jerk off and cum together like normal fucking people?"

"Because that's boring." His words thundered down upon me. There was something so incredibly sexy and equally as maddening about the power he had over me. "You cum first, you lose. Got it?"

"What the hell does the loser lose, anyway?"

Jerking us harder, faster, he leaned in and said, "If you cum first, I don't move in. You lose me as your roommate."

That's not fucking fair! He'd been sucking my cock for the last—however long. I already had a huge head start. I could cum any second, and he only just then started jerking. "Not happening, no."

"Better hold off, then," he teased, staring down at me, pressing his power onto me. His fist was making quick work of my edged, sensitive, wet and slick-as-fuck cock. There was no way I'd be able to hold back when I reached the brink. My loss and his "victory" was certain.

"I have better stakes for you," I retorted. I would do everything in my power to focus on our words and, with every fiber of my weak, vulnerable body, ignore the pulsing pleasure downstairs. "Far, far better, far higher stakes."

"Too late."

"Not too late. I haven't accepted your terms." I propped myself up with my elbows so as to get into his face more, my own eyes squinting with conviction. "If you cum first, you gotta kiss me."

His jerking stopped, his eyes went queer, then he resumed again. "Kiss?" he said, as if he actually didn't hear me right.

"Yeah, the mouth, full on. Like we're nasty, clothes-off, don't-give-a-fuck lovers. You gotta put your lips all over mine."

"No fucking way."

"Yes. That's what's at stake. You want *my* stakes to be my losing you as a roommate? Fine. Sounds a bit like your loss too, but if you insist so badly, then there's my stakes. Roommate, or kiss? Kiss, or roommate?"

He swallowed. I watched his throat, watched as he swallowed hard. *I have him*, I thought. *I have him right where I want him.*

He kept jerking and jerking and jerking, and I said, "Thinking about it, now?" I smiled, watching the emotions battle across his face. "Oh, fuck. Can you imagine? If you actually ... *lost?* Think about what you'd have to do. Think about ... think about what you'd be *forced* to do, if you cum first. Putting your lips all over mine. Kissing me like a boyfriend. How fucking horrible that'd be, huh? How humiliating. How *degrading*."

His breath became audible. *Is this turning him on?* Andrew Knudson, half-moaning as he jerked the both of us. His legs began to shake; I could feel the muscles in them as they tremored through my own. His eyebrows screwed upward, the folds of his forehead showing. He parted his mouth, his head thrown back as his breathing became less air and more voice ... a whimper, a cry ...

"Better hold off," I whispered at him.

And then he came. The jerking on my cock stopped and a rope of his cum landed across my chest, white and heavy. Another

followed, less powerful. Then a third and a
fourth, and he kept pulling and pulling on his
cock, but gentler now, and his eyes were closed
in a quiet, blissful agony.

Winner.

Then he laid down—or rather, fell—onto
the bed beside me. His hand still gripped his
cock, but his other one let go of mine as his
arm folded into my body like an eagle's wing.
One might almost say he were cuddling into
me.

His chest heaved, exhaling heavily after
the mighty orgasm. Every puff of air from his
mouth landed hot against my face, and I
realized belatedly that I was smiling.

*I made Andrew Knudson do that. That was all
me.*

Watching him breathe, in and out, in and
out, I suddenly found my strength. I rushed in
and put my lips against his. At first he froze,
even his breathing stopped. His whole body
went rigid at the touch of my lips to his. Then,
I let my lips become gentle. I didn't want to

force the kiss on him, not anymore; I wanted his permission. Even without words, I requested permission to go on.

His lips, ever slowly, parted to receive mine. Then his tongue darted out, tickled my lips with seeming encouragement, letting me in.

Permission granted.

Then quite suddenly, he seemed to forget all about the mess he just made across my chest, or the cum dribbling from his still-perky cock, and he found new breath in our feverish kisses.

I regarded the cum just as little, a light and silent laughter fluttering in my chest as I wrestled tongue and mouth with the boy of my dreams in my messy dorm bed.

If I'd known a stupid project in Intro to Psych was going to lead to this ...

Winning never felt so good.

His mouth almost hurt, at times too intense for me, pressing strongly against mine, pushing teeth and tongue and warm, wetted lips ... and then it would grow gentle. For a moment, I couldn't keep up. In the next moment, I was the one in charge, controlling his lips and leading the kiss.

It was a delicate dance of breaths and mouths.

That night, he slept in my bed. The lover's mess between us probably dried, and whatever sort of permanent stains it would cause, I literally did not care. Andrew held me like a lover, whether he'd ever admit that or not, and I felt the long drawl of a sleeper's breathing against my cheek for hours and hours and hours.

I was happy. The TV's murmur went on, my roommate never came back, and I was happy.

But that's twice now that I've found a reward in deceiving Andrew: once during our what-are-you-thinking game when I lied to win, and this time with offering him beer. Which, if either, was a necessary evil, and what, if neither, could I have done otherwise?

The game is played many ways, and in its end, we should both come out winners, shouldn't we?

[9]

"A," Andrew asks me, "or B?"

This brings us back to our little study game of guess-the-right-bone. "A for absolutely horny, B for boner," I reply wittily, squirming.

He puts a foot on the bed, an elbow propped on his knee, and leans over my restrained body to say, "A for agony, B for belt." Then he snapped the belt in his grip for punctuation, sobering me.

Over the course of our year as roommates,

the dorm game has taken a turn for the scary. Now that he's around me all the time—and, being his roommate, I have nowhere really to hide—he has introduced me to a score of alternative and vastly worse consequences for wrong answers, laughably small ways to reward me for right answers, and an arsenal of wicked items with which to inflict joyful, frustrating, and oftentimes surprising torment on me.

I learned it wasn't the pain he enjoyed; he was, so he claimed, not really a sadist. It wasn't the pain that ever turned him on. It was the thrill of the win and the reward—or the loss and the humiliating punishment that followed.

"Were you ever bullied as a kid?" I ask him, my feet twirling around playfully, pulling against the sock-binds that had them so bound to the bed. "And more pressingly, are these socks clean? I've been concerned about that ever since you used them to tie up my hands and feet, seriously ..."

"Yeah, about as clean as they get after one of my four-hour workouts," he says, moving over me and baring the worst of his forceful stares onto me. "That might explain the man-stink of them. You like my man-stink?"

"When it's yours," I say, smiling sweetly. "Not so much your *socks'* stink."

"Learn to love it. You get this next question wrong and I'm tying those socks to your face when you sleep tonight." I blanch, rolling my eyes. "You will learn to love every part of me whether it makes you sick or not."

"Love?" I screw my eyes back onto him, lifting a brow. "Love, did you just say? Andrew, is this your way of confessing the 'L' word to me?"

He tosses the belt onto the other bed, suddenly choosing to ditch it, I guess. "Change of plan. Wrong answer's earning you a tickle."

Fuck. I hate his tickles. I hate them so, so, so fucking bad because he's so *good* at it. The last time he gave me a harsh tickling, we had a complaint from the R.A. who had to come to

our room to tell us to keep down the noise—
the noise being: my hysterical screaming and
laughing and begging Andrew to stop. Why
does he have to be into weird shit like tickling
and sock-sniffing and questions and betting
and jerkoff-races and belt-flogging and
stripping games and fuck-knows-what-else?

"A," he says, the flashcard pinched
between an eager forefinger and thumb, "or
B?"

"I don't even remember what the choices
were," I complain. "What's the name for *which*
bone in the body?"

"In the hand," he answers. "And if you
weren't paying attention to the choices, not
my problem. You're fucked. A or B?"

"How does that help me learn? This whole
thing is supposed to be about me *learning*," I
argue back, my blood rising. Quite suddenly,
in fact, I find my face flushing with the long-
pent-up anger and sexual frustration spawned
by Andrew, master tormentor and owner of
my fucking soul. "You do this for *your*

entertainment. You don't give a shit if I fail or pass any of my classes. You never gave a shit, not since Intro to Psych, not since ever. Hell, you wouldn't give a deep-fried fuck if I flunked outta school, wasted all my scholarships, drew a noose around my neck ... just as long as we keep playing your stupid fucking dorm game."

"Wrong answer," he says, as if he can't tell how angry I've suddenly gotten, as if he let every word of my impassioned spiel go unheard.

And then he's on me. I cry out, shocked because I was genuinely not expecting him to go through with tickling me. But really, why the fuck am I surprised? I scream at once as his fingers dig into my exposed armpits. I pull and pull against the socks that are tied so tight at my wrists and ankles, pulling and yanking until I'm quite sure one or all of my appendages are likely to break.

"GET THE FUCK OFF!" I scream, howling with noises that land somewhere between agony and joyous unintended laughter.

"You love it," he says, his fingers unrelenting. "You love it so much. A or B, the choice was simple," he goes on, unworried, casual as a boy with his feet kicked up on a desk while he makes sweet torment of his roommate beneath his sinful fingers. "Tickling's the punishment, I was pretty fucking clear. But oh no, you preferred to just talk and talk and talk ..."

The sock at my right ankle pulls loose. I thrash my right foot, kicking, but I can't get him off me. Then the hands seem to come loose at once, and in a movement that's so fast I can't see it, I've punched Andrew square in the face.

He falls back, tumbling off the bed and landing on the carpet.

I sit up, alarmed. He puts a hand up to his nose, finds it bleeding. Quickly, he gets to his feet and turns away, bringing his hands to his nose to stop the bleeding. I'm staring in horror at Andrew as he moves to the box of tissues at the desk, pulls a fistful and brings them to his face.

"Oh fuck," I exclaim, a hand of my own going to my mouth. "Andrew. I'm so fucking sorry. I just, I was just ... You were tickling me and I ..."

My left ankle's still tied to the bedpost and all the aching and pain of being tickled is gone in an instant. Andrew's naked backside is all that exists.

"Andrew, please, say something. You okay?"

"Yep," is all he says.

I stare at him for a while. He doesn't move, just standing there with his back turned, pushing tissue after tissue into his face. I notice a handful he sets on the desk—notice the amount of blood drenching them. *Fuck*, I think, studying the wad in horror. *I hit him really hard.*

"Andrew?"

"Right in the nose," he grunts. "Won't

stop bleeding," he adds, but it sounds more like an observation, less like a complaint. He's trying not to sound hurt, I realize. He's acting all manly, all you-didn't-hurt-me, all no-big-deal ... but his nose is basically pouring blood, right?

"Andrew."

Suddenly he goes for the bathroom, says, "I'm alright," just before shutting the door behind him. The faucet turns on. It's all I can hear now.

I grab at the sock at my left ankle, untie it, and free myself from the bed. Suddenly ashamed of my outburst, I don't feel right being all naked anymore. I fetch a shirt off the ground, slip it over my head, and pull a pair of boxers on. Quickly, I move to the bathroom door and press my ear to it.

"Andrew?"

He doesn't respond. I close my eyes to listen better. Through the running water, I hear tissues crinkling. I hear the water breaking, perhaps with his hands plunging into its gushing stream. Maybe he's taken to a washcloth or a towel. Did I break his nose? What the fuck did I do?

"Say you're going to be fine," I call through the door, desperate and helpless.

After a moment too long, I hear: "Gonna be fine."

"Tell me you're going to be fine and *mean* it. Tell me if you're *not* going to be fine, either, please. Do I ... Should we ... Should I call the campus medics or—?"

"No."

"Alright." I pull away from the door. Maybe I'm overreacting. I have no fucking idea. I've never hit anyone before. Not even in high school, or elementary school, never. The impact of my knuckles against his face, I can't even remember it. My hand throbs a bit, but I can't tell if it's from being restrained or if it was from the impact of my bones hitting the beautiful face of my roommate, Andrew Knudson.

Flashcards season the floor, answered right

or wrong, forgotten. I pick up the last one he'd asked me, read it with absent eyes. *A, I see. The answer was A.* I wonder if I can name the possible bones I could've broken in my hand ... in my wrist. The bones I could've broken in his face.

I sit on the bed and wait.

Only four minutes later, the bathroom door opens and Andrew emerges. He plops down on his bed, stares at the floor. A tiny wad of toilet paper is shoved into either nostril and he stares at the floor listlessly, emotionlessly, a big muscled troll turned to stone.

"You alright?" I ask quietly.

"Yeah," he says. He seems to be just staring at the flashcards on the ground, or staring through them, or staring at nothing at all.

"I'm sorry I hit you."

"Maybe the games are stupid," he says back.

"They're not always stupid," I reason.

He's still staring at the floor; his eyes won't meet mine. *Maybe he's embarrassed. Maybe he's ashamed too.* "I mean, sometimes they're really hot. I just wonder sometimes if ..." I trail off, unsure how to put it. The air conditioner comes on, fills the room with a gentle, unassuming hum. I don't welcome it, shivering against the sudden draft that now kicks through my already quite chilly room.

"I can find another dorm," he says.

I stammer. "N-No, Andrew. You don't have to move out. That's kind of ... That's kind of an overreaction, really."

His eyes flick to the other side of the room. He still won't look at me. *Comfort him,* I tell myself. *He needs your reassurance.* "There's nothing wrong with you, Andrew. I ... I think we're actually—you and I, we actually have a lot in common."

He plucks out the tissues, sniffs, then looks back at the flashcards on the floor. It's so strange, for someone with so much cockiness and dominance and power to be so in need of comfort.

I stand, cross the room and lower myself next to him on his bed. He turns his head slightly, but still won't meet my eyes. "Andrew ..."

Ever since the day I got him drunk and earned a tongue-wrestling session from him, his lips have yet to meet mine again. Maybe the craving for an honest, genuine, physically-loving relationship between us has driven me somewhat mad, and I'm lashing out at him for not giving me what I need.

"You meant all that," he states suddenly.

I look at him, confused. "What do you mean?"

"All that about me not caring about you. That the only thing I care about is the playing. That I don't ... That I wouldn't care if, like, you flunked all your classes, or ... or ..." He bites his lip and squints at the floor pensively.

"Well, I didn't say it to hurt you," I point out. "I just ... I just meant that, sometimes, I want ..." A sigh escapes my lips. Maybe I shouldn't have said a thing at all. I mean, really, is it *that* bad what we have? The hottest guy on campus is my roommate and he's constantly wanting to put me in situations that get one or both of our clothes off somehow, and oftentimes it involves him or I jerking off or being jerked off. Maybe there's nothing wrong with him at all; maybe it's something wrong with me.

"I care about you."

I study the side of his face, surprised. "What?"

"I care about you," he repeats. "So, like ... tell me what it is you want from me."

His blue eyes are so intense, even looking at them from the side, I can still feel his influence. *If you only knew what I want.* Maybe this is another of his games. But really, when you think of it, isn't kinda everything in life a game? Whether you win a friendship by saying the right thing, or lose a lover by saying it all wrong? Whether you score the job by wowing your interviewer, by dressing the part, by winning yet another game? When does the playing stop? At what age do we graduate from playing games with one another and, instead, reap the benefits of all our years' rewards and lessons and personal triumphs?

"I just want to know what we are," I tell him.

"We're roommates."

"We're so, so ... *so* much more than that, Andrew."

"Why? Because we get naked and do stuff? Because I have certain sexual interests and, like ..." He swallows hard, presses his lips together before forming his next words. "I don't see why we gotta call it something. Why the fuck's a person gotta be straight or gay. Lovers or friends. Why the fuck?"

"Just makes it easier for me, I guess." I place a hand on his thigh. His gaze shifts, now focused quite intently on my innocent hand. "I guess calling us something is a game in and of itself, don't you think? Except ... it isn't required to have any rules. I don't want a rule telling me when I can kiss you or—"

I close my eyes. I've said it. *I want to kiss you, Andrew Fucking Knudson. I want to kiss you and I want you to kiss me and, just for this moment, I don't want alcohol or belts or flashcards or dominance involved.*

That's when I feel his lips touch mine. With my eyes closed, I feel his mouth open and a tongue greets my lips, traces them, tickles them.

I open my mouth to his, and the heat between us becomes one. When I breathe, he breathes, and our heads tilt gently as we kiss. Even our noses seem to kiss—lightly, of course, minding the ache that surely still lives in his—and our faces caress one another, mouths attached, tongues greeting.

When at last we part, I confess. "I cheated on our first game. The thought game. You'd gotten what I was thinking right and I lied and said you were wrong." He lifts his brows in mock surprise. "I just wanted to see you naked so badly."

Unsmiling, he regards my anxious face for a long, agonized moment. Then, finally: "We'll make a new game of it," he offers. "Rule is, when you want me naked, you just ask. When you want to kiss me, you just fucking go for it."

Even this little offering of his, he makes it sound like an order, his voice strong as stone. My thighs squeeze together. I wonder if one of the many flashcards on the floor includes the bone that's now formed between my legs.

"Your terms are accepted," I say. Then, as prompted, I fucking go for it, crashing my lips into his. The hand I'd so strategically placed on his thigh, I let it gently slide between his legs.

He responds with a sigh of pleasure.

Feeling smart, I push him down into the bed and climb over his body like a beast. Yeah, *I'm* the beast now. Mounting Andrew, I make quick work of his face, my hand opening up his clothes below to claim my prize—all seven inches of it. It's my turn now to part lips and bathe his cock with my tongue, generously. I open my mouth to him, one inch of him in, two inches, three. He quivers under my grip, and I feel a moan cascading down his body. My hands reach up, desperate, grabbing, and as I swallow and tongue and suck his seven inches of glory, my hands discover his rippling abs as if for the first time. My hands discover his pecs, making a game out of his left nipple, then his right. Grabbing his hips and rocking myself up and down, I put Andrew where I want him and nowhere else.

I give him no choice but to enjoy it.

And when he cums, the thunder from his voice shakes the walls. For now, Andrew is under my control. I'm the one whose game we're playing tonight. And in my game, there are never losers.

Printed in Great Britain
by Amazon